The Mystery of RACKETY'S WAY

By Margaret Friskey

Illustrations by Frances Eckart

CHILDRENS PRESS, Chicago

Library of Congress Catalog Card Number: 69-14687

4 5 6 7 8 9 10 11 12 13 14 15 16 17 18 19 20 21 22 23 24 25 R 75 74 73 72

Hush and Shush were
two little rabbits.

They were as quiet
as balls of fur under
a bush.

Crash! Bang!

They heard their
noisy brother coming.

Twigs snapped as
Rackety Rabbit jumped
into the nest.

"Something has happened
to our meadow," he said.
"Just listen."
"How can we hear anything
when you are making so much
noise?" asked Hush.
Rackety was quiet.
They listened.

They heard zzz-zzz, zzz-zzz.

"A man is sawing wood," said
Rackety.

They heard bang-bang, bang-bang.

"A man is pounding nails,"
said Rackety. "They are building
a people-house in our meadow."

Hush said, "We live in this
meadow with a frog on a log, a
fat groundhog, two squirrels and
three chipmunks. We can live
with people, too."

Then the three little rabbits
heard something else.
It made their ears stand
straight up.

RUFF-RUFF

The air shook with sound.
The three little rabbits
peeked out of the nest.
They saw a great big dog.
He was ENORMOUS.
"A big dog at the people-
house can spoil everything
for us rabbits," said Rackety.

"We must move," said Hush.

"Where?" asked Rackety.

"I remember a good place," said Shush. "It is a beautiful park. A sign on the gate says, ZOO — NO DOGS."

"Can we find it?" asked Hush. "It is a long way from this meadow."

"I will ask the squirrels
which way to go," said Rackety.
"The squirrels know everything."

"Which way is the zoo?" asked Rackety.

"Climb a tree. You can see from the top of a tree which way to go," said the squirrels.

"Rabbits can't climb trees," said Rackety.

"Then hop to the big tree. Turn left. Hop to the brook."

"Then what?" asked Rackety.

"Then ask the frog which way to go," said the squirrels.

Hush and Shush and Rackety
hopped to the big tree. They
turned left, and hopped to the
brook. They did not see the big
dog. But they heard him barking.

They saw the frog on a log.

"Which way is the zoo?"
asked Rackety.

"Swim across the brook,"
said the frog. "Then ask the
chipmunks."

"Rabbits can't swim," said
Rackety.

"Then do this," said the
frog.
"Move back a little way.
Run a few steps. And jump."

The rabbits moved back a
little way and jumped.
They landed in the mud
at the edge of the brook.

"We did not listen to the frog," said Hush. He shook the mud off his feet. "We forgot to run a few steps."

They tried again. This time they jumped across the brook.

They did not see the
chipmunks.

"I wish we could fly,"
said Hush. "Then we could
see which way to go."

"Rabbits can't fly," said
Rackety. "I will go and find
the chipmunks."

Rackety did not hear the dog.
But he almost bumped into him.
The dog was walking along
with his nose to the ground.
Rackety tiptoed away as
quietly as he could.

"Whee!" said Rackety and he
whistled through his teeth with
fright.

"Which way is the zoo?" he
asked when he found the chipmunks.
"We never go to the zoo,"
said the chipmunks. "But the dog
goes — as far as the gate. He
follows his nose to get there."

Rackety ran back to Hush and
Shush.

"Maybe rabbits can't climb
or swim or fly," said Rackety.
"But rabbits have noses. We
will follow our noses to the zoo."

Off they went, three different
ways, after three different noses.

Hush and Shush and Rackety
sat down to rest.

"What makes you so tired?"
asked the fat groundhog.

"We have tried and tried to get to the zoo," said Rackety. "And that stupid dog makes us tired. He follows his nose to the zoo. But we cannot."

"He is not stupid," said the groundhog. "A dog has a keen sense of smell. His nose tells him which way to go."

"Rabbits can't smell things as a dog does," said Rackety. "They can't climb or swim or fly."

"You must have something special," said the groundhog. "Everyone does. Why it's your ears! Rabbits have wonderful ears."

"We can follow our ears!
We can follow our ears!"
shouted Rackety hopping up
and down.

"But look at your ears,"
said Hush. "One points left
and one points right."

"Let's think this over,"
said Shush. "We have come a
long way, but have not found
the zoo."

They were as quiet as
butterflies on the grass.

As rabbits do, they quietly
turned their long ears this
way and that way.

Suddenly they heard an
elephant trumpet. They heard
a peacock screech.

"The zoo!" said Rackety.
"It's over there. That way."

"Of course," said Hush.
"We follow the sounds our
ears hear."

In no time at all the three
rabbits had crawled under the
fence around the zoo.

Rackety scattered some stones
as he jumped across a path in the
park where there were no dogs.

Let squirrels climb, frogs swim,
birds fly, and dogs follow noses!
The rabbits knew that they, too,
had something special.

Doesn't everyone?